Your Mommy Is My Bestie

Casey Baker

AuthorHouse™
1663 Liberty Drive
Bloomington, IN 47403
www.authorhouse.com
Phone: 1 (800) 839-8640

ISBN: 978-1-7283-3273-4 (sc)
ISBN: 978-1-7283-3272-7 (e)

Library of Congress Control Number: 2019916806

Print information available on the last page.

Published by AuthorHouse 10/22/2019

authorHOUSE®

For my best friend Heather and
her amazing son Weston

Your mommy is my bestie, I just wanted you to know. She always dreamed of having you to love and to hold.

We dreamed of having babies that would grow up to be close. Just like your mom and me, we wanted that the most.

Your mom came over one day and I could see it in her eyes. She had a secret. A wonderful, big, important surprise.

The important secret was that God had given her you— yes you! We were so happy! Yahoo! Yahoo!

The days had passed and your mommy's belly grew. Some day you would be here, brand spanking new.

It's hard to be patient waiting for you to be here. We've waited for what seems like forever for you my dear.

The day has finally come and you've made your big debut. Our hearts are full, so full you see. We are so happy too.

Before you steal your mommy's whole heart I just needed you to know. Your mommy is the greatest, with a heart as pure as gold.

I was her bestie first, there's no changing that you see. However it's clear priorities change, and you're more important than me.

I'll always be here for you and your mommy any day. An adopted Auntie you can count on in any sort of way.

I love you both from the bottom of my heart. Days we aren't together we will never be apart.

I just needed you to know and I wanted you to see. Just how important you and your mom are to me.

I'll always love you dearly and your mommy so you see. Besties until the end of time, that's your mommy and me.

Printed in the United States
By Bookmasters